The Disobedient Eels

and Other Italian Tales

The
Disobedient Eels

and Other Italian Tales

by Maria Cimino

with pictures by Claire Nivola

Pantheon Books

Typography by Harriett Banner

For my father

---

remembering
how he used to tell
these tales

The Disobedient Eels

and Other Italian Tales

The Disobedient Eels

The city of Chioggia lies not too far from Venice. The fishermen there are handsome, strong, and hard-working. But they are simple-minded too, according to Venetian gondoliers who tell this story.

One day a fisherman from Chioggia came to Venice with a basketful of eels. Wanting to get across a canal, he asked what the fare was.

"Five cents a head," said the ferryman.

"Oh, that's too much for all these heads," said the fisherman, looking at his basket.

"Into the water, my dear eels. It's swimming across for you. I'll wait on the other side."

He emptied his basket into the canal, paid

his fare, and was across in no time. Then he
sat down on the landing to wait for his eels.

He waited, calling out now and then, "Hey,
eels! Where are you? Why are you so long in
getting here? Come on, swim this way!"

And gondoliers say that he is still sitting
there waiting for his eels.

The Fat Man

A fat man was on his way to Sorrento in the days when the city had gates. It was late and he walked as fast as he could, afraid that he would find the gates closed for the night. Puffing hard, he came upon a farmer on the road.

"Do you think I'll get in?" he asked.

The farmer looked him over carefully.

"Well," he answered, "a cartload of hay can make it. Maybe you can."

The Wise Judge

A merchant from Bari was going on a pilgrimage to Rome and he left three hundred gold pieces in the care of a friend.

"Here," he said. "Hold these for me. I am going to Rome. If I do not return within the year, use the money for prayers for my soul.

If I return before the year is up, give me back whatever you like. Keep the rest for yourself."

He went to Rome and was back well within the year. When he asked for his money the friend said, "According to our agreement?"

"Of course," said the pilgrim.

"Here, then. Ten gold pieces for you and two hundred and ninety for me."

The pilgrim crossed himself. "Is this how you are to be trusted? Pocketing what is mine?"

"Not at all," said the friend smoothly. "If you think I am wrong, let's go before the court."

The judge listened to both sides. Then he said to the friend, "Give the pilgrim the two hundred and ninety pieces of gold you are holding. The pilgrim will give you the ten pieces you gave him.

"According to the terms of your agreement you were to return to him whatever you liked. Evidently it is the two hundred and ninety pieces that you like. Now return them to their owner. Keep for yourself the amount you do not want—ten gold pieces."

The Silent Wife

The women of Florence are great talkers—so people say. But there was one man in that city who had a wife who never spoke. No matter what he said or what he did she was always silent.

He set himself to find a way to make her talk.

First he made her a pair of little leather shoes. He made them so tight he was sure she would call out in pain when she put them on. But no! There was not a sound out of her.

Next he made her a long leather skirt. It was so long and tight she could hardly move when she put it on. It was no use. She still remained dumb.

At last he decided to pretend he was dead and see whether that would work. So he lay down on the bed, looking for all the world as if he had just died.

When the wife came in and saw him she burst out stammering, "Oh, my d-dear husband—the shoes so t-tight, the skirt so l-long and t-tight—and now you have gone and d-died, leaving me all alone. W-what shall I do?"

"I see you have found your voice at last," said the husband as he sat up laughing. "And now I know! *You stammer!*"

The husband soon wished he had left well enough alone. From then on she never stopped talking and stammering, and there was no more peace in that house.

A Good Guesser

Two farmers met on a country road. One said to the other, "Do you know, we have a new baby at our house."

"Well, good luck! Don't tell me. Let me guess. It's a little boy."

"No."

"Then, a little girl."

"Bravo, however did you guess it?"

The Talking Boat

Bara Piero was a fisherman who lived on the little island of Burano just off the Grand Canal of Venice. His fishing boat was his living, but it was more than that. He looked on it as his best friend. Every evening he would stroll to the dock and say, "Good evening, my dear boat."

On Burano there also lived a young fisherman called Donao who wanted to marry Bara Piero's daughter. One evening Donao met Bara Piero on his usual walk and asked him if he could marry his daughter.

"Well—someday, perhaps, my son," said Bara Piero, "but do you think marrying my daughter is like borrowing a loaf of bread? Whoever gets my daughter Beta must own a boat and be a good fisherman." And he went on his way without another word.

The next time Donao met Bara Piero the first thing he said was that he was saving his money to buy a boat.

"Good for you," said the old man. And he walked off as if he had forgotten all about the marriage.

Then and there Donao decided that he would remind him of it in such a way that he would never forget. The following evening Donao hid in the bottom of Bara Piero's boat.

Pretty soon, along came Bara Piero on his evening stroll. As usual he stopped at the dock.

"Good evening, my dear boat," he said.

"A very good evening to you, Bara Piero," answered the boat.

"What's that!" cried Bara Piero, taken aback. "Look, now even a boat talks." Then bracing himself, he cried, "Who are you—god or devil? Answer me!"

"Neither," said the boat. "I am an angel sent from heaven to bid you give your daughter to Donao in marriage."

"Ah...now I see what's going on here," said Bara Piero. "Very well, my dear boat. Tell Donao that he has my consent."

And he went on to finish his stroll.

Nero and the Old Woman

Once when Nero, Emperor of Rome, was walking alone on a country road he met an old woman.

"Where are you going?" he asked her.

"Oh, I'm out looking for a crust of bread," she answered.

"Poor old woman," said Nero. "These are hard times. They say this Nero is a wicked king."

"May God grant him a long life," said the old woman.

"Why do you say that?" said Nero. "Why do you wish him well when everybody else in Rome is cursing him?"

Now the old woman had no idea that she was talking to Nero himself.

"Kind sir," she said. "It's true Nero is a wicked king. But I have lived a long time. I have seen plenty of the misery that comes from the wickedness of selfish kings.

"I remember we had a king once, he was bad. Then we had another, he was worse. As for the third king, he was the worst of all.

"Now we have this Nero. He is even more cruel and wicked than those three kings put together. Yet I say, 'God bless him and keep him, and save us all from the next king.' "

Thirty Reasons

A man in need of money went to his friend.

"Listen," he said, "can you lend me one hundred *lire*?"

"One hundred *lire*?" said the friend. "I'm terribly sorry but I can't, for thirty reasons. The first is that I haven't got one hundred *lire*. The second is…"

"Stop! The first is all I need. Never mind the rest."

Or Else . . . .

There was a big rough-looking fellow who went around begging for his living. Whenever he met anyone walking alone he would stop, and cupping his hand over his mouth he would whisper, "A penny for the poor, or else..."

Frightened, they would throw him a coin and hurry on. He even knocked at people's doors begging for "a penny, or else."

Now there lived in this town a woman who was so scared of the beggar that she told her husband he must do something about it.

"Leave it to me," he said. "I'll settle it once and for all."

That day when the beggar came on his rounds and the wife opened the door, he whispered in his usual way, "A penny for the poor, or else..."

"Or else...or else what?" roared the woman's husband as he jumped out from behind the kitchen door.

"Or else...? Or else I'll go away," said the beggar meekly. And off he went.

The Stubborn Farmer

A farmer was going down to Biella. The weather was so bad it was hard to make headway on the road. But he had important business in town, and he bowed his head against the rain and the tempest and went forward.

By and by he met an old man who said, "Good morning, where are you going in such a hurry?"

"To Biella," said the farmer without stopping.

"You could at least say 'God willing.'"

The farmer stopped, looked the old man straight in the eye and retorted, "God willing or no, I am going to Biella."

Now that old man was the Lord himself, and he said, "My friend, it will be seven years before you see Biella. Jump into that swamp and stay there seven years."

The farmer turned into a frog on the spot, gave one jump, and landed in the swamp.

Seven years passed. The farmer came out of the swamp, became a man, put on his hat, and once more started for Biella. He had gone only a few steps when there was that old man again.

"Where are you going now, my good man?"

"To Biella."

"You could say 'God willing.' "

"If God wills it, good. If not, I am quite able to go into the swamp on my own."

And there was no getting any more out of him.

Another Good Guesser

A peasant met his friend coming out of a vineyard carrying a covered basket.

"I see you have been to the vineyard," he
said. "What have you got in that basket you're
carrying?"

"If you can guess I'll give you a bunch."

"Well…is it grapes?"

"You must be a magician. That's just what
I have in this basket."

And he gave his friend half the grapes he
was taking to his master.

No Deal

In Sicily every town considers its own patron saint better than any other. Once a man was visiting a fair in a neighboring town. He stopped to look at some figures in the booth of a vendor of images. He chose a fine little figure of Saint Agata, patron saint of his own town, and a slightly larger one of Saint Venere, the local saint.

"How much?" he asked.

"One for Saint Agata, two for our Saint Venere," said the vendor.

"Good," said the man. "One plus two makes three. Here are three pennies. But I am paying you two for our Saint Agata and one for your Saint Venere."

"In that case it's no deal," said the vendor. "It's either one for Saint Agata and two for Saint Venere, or nothing!" And he put the saints back on the shelf.

The Case Against the Flies

Giufá bought a fine piece of veal for his dinner. He left it on the kitchen table and went out to do another errand. When he came back the meat was gone. The flies had eaten it all up.

He went to the judge, demanding justice against the flies who had eaten up his dinner. The judge smiled faintly.

"You have reason to complain," he said. "From now on you must kill every fly you see."

Just then a fly settled on the judge's nose. Giufá jumped up and dealt the fly such a blow that it resounded through the entire room.

"You dog," screamed the judge. "What's the matter with you? Explain your action."

Giufá calmly replied, "Your honor, I was just following your advice and went after the fly that settled on your nose. It's dead now."

It, Him, or Me

A man captured by pirates was taken to Tripoli and sold into slavery. Caught in a misdeed, he was then condemned to die. When the guards were taking him to his execution they passed an elephant on the road.

"If I weren't going to my death, I would teach that elephant to talk," he said.

The guards reported this to their master. Curious to hear an elephant talk, he suspended sentence and ordered them to bring the slave before him again.

"Is it true that you can teach an elephant to talk?" said the master.

"Yes," answered the man.

"How long would it take?"

"Ten years."

"And if you don't succeed?"

"Send me to whatever death you choose," said the man.

"Very well," said the master.

That night another slave said, "What if you fail? At the end of ten years they'll kill you."

"In ten years it will be it or him or me," said the man.

"What do you mean?"

"Either the elephant will die, or the master, or I. Meantime nothing will be lost. And who can tell? Maybe the elephant will learn to talk."

Money Talks

One morning when Gianni was leaving for the market a friend called out to him.

"Hey, Gianni," he said. "Do me a favor. Buy me a guitar at the market."

Gianni nodded and went to the market, and forgot all about it.

The next day, the same thing—Gianni forgot to buy the guitar. "Oh, what a fool I am," he said.

It went on this way for a while, the friend asking for a guitar and Gianni forgetting to buy it. Until one fine morning when Gianni was starting for the market, his friend came running.

"Hey, Gianni. Here's one hundred *lire*. Please buy me that guitar. And don't forget this time."

"Ah, my dear friend," said Gianni. "Now I see that you really intend to play the guitar."

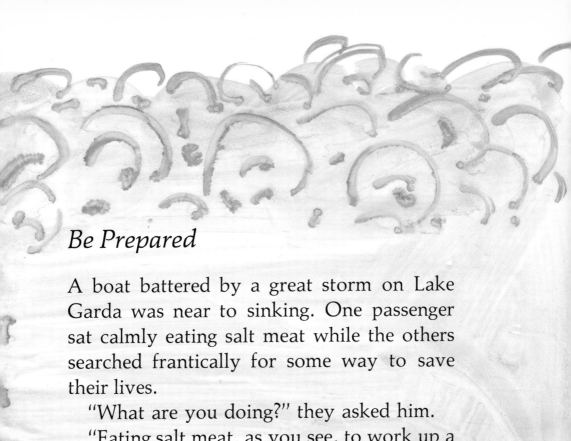

Be Prepared

A boat battered by a great storm on Lake Garda was near to sinking. One passenger sat calmly eating salt meat while the others searched frantically for some way to save their lives.

"What are you doing?" they asked him.

"Eating salt meat, as you see, to work up a thirst," he said. "Soon I may have to drink a lot of water."

Wait for the Sheep

Prince Azzolino had a storyteller in his household for the long winter evenings. One night when the storyteller was about to go to bed the Prince asked for a tale. And although he could hardly keep his eyes open the storyteller began.

"Once there was a peasant who had saved one hundred gold pieces and he went to the market to buy sheep. He got two sheep for each piece of money and started for home driving two hundred sheep ahead of him. When he came to the shallow stream he had crossed on his way to market, he found that a sudden heavy rain had swelled it into a river. On the shore was a poor fisherman in his little boat.

"The peasant borrowed the boat to get his sheep across. It was so small that it could hold only one sheep besides the peasant. He began

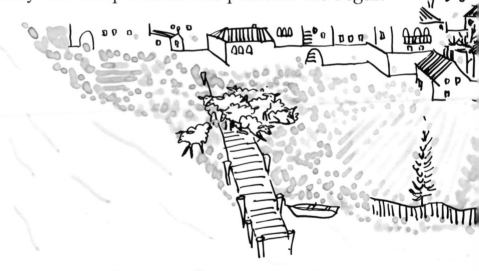

to row the first sheep across. The river was wide. He rowed across and put the sheep ashore. He rowed back and got another sheep. Again and again. Back and forth. Back and forth."

The storyteller stopped. He was almost asleep.

"Go on," said the Prince, shaking him.

The storyteller opened one eye and answered, "Let all the sheep get across first. Then I'll tell you the rest. In the meantime we may as well get some sleep."

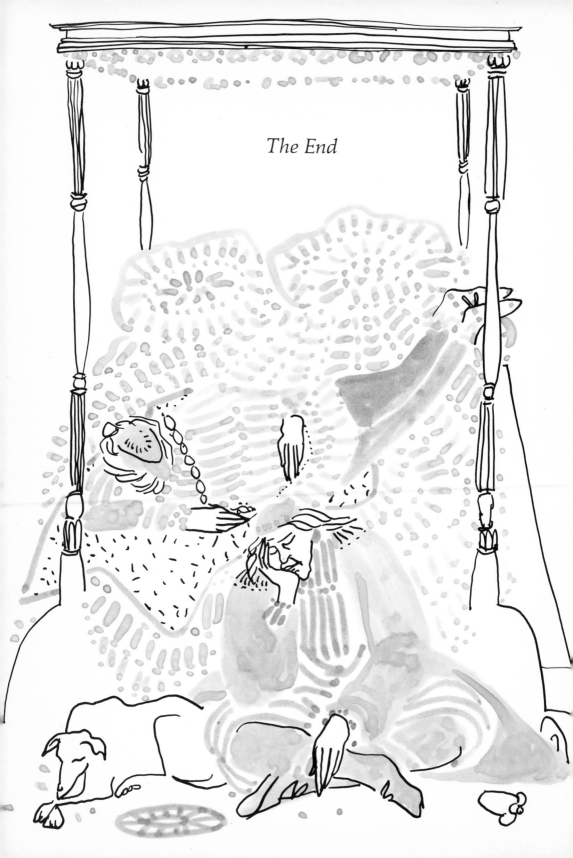

The End